Hartford Fire Insurance Company

Christmas Souvenir 1893

Hartford Fire Insurance Company

Christmas Souvenir 1893

ISBN/EAN: 9783337380236

Printed in Europe, USA, Canada, Australia, Japan

Cover: Foto ©Andreas Hilbeck / pixelio.de

More available books at **www.hansebooks.com**

CHRISTMAS
SOUVENIR
1893

HARTFORD · FIRE · INSURANCE
COMPANY · HARTFORD · CONN.

GENEVIEVE.

Have you seen a little maiden,
  Quaint and sweet and very fair—
Violets blooming in her eyes
('Twas in spring she left the skies),
  Sunbeams playing in her hair—
Ay, a bonnie sprite from Aiden?
  'Tis our darling, Genevieve!

Have you seen a little fairy,
  Weaving web and woof of bliss
O'er the dwelling where she bides—
Where her winsome spirit glides—
  Brewing here and there a kiss,
When her tiny footsteps tarry?
  'Tis our Queenie, Genevieve!

Have you seen among the roses,
    One rare bud outvie the rest—
All its heart a wondrous pearl?
She it is—our little girl;
    Pearl of pearls; Love's high bequest,
Sweetest floweret 'midst the posies,
    Heart's-ease—pansy, Genevieve!

Have you seen this little maiden,
    In the sunshine—by the way,
Mignon that we love so well,
Child or angel, who can tell?
(She may child to others be,
She is angel unto me.)
    Heaven guard her night and day,
All her life with joy be laden,
    Mamma's treasure, Genevieve.

H, why should the spirit of
    mortal be proud?
Like a swift-fleeting meteor, a fast-
    flying cloud,
A flash of the lightning, a break of
    the wave,
Man passeth from life to his rest in
    the grave.

The leaves of the oak and the willow shall fade,
Be scattered around and together be laid;
And the young and the old, and the low and the high,
Shall moulder to dust and together shall lie.

HE infant a mother attended
      and loved;
   The mother that infant's affec-
      tion who proved;
The husband that mother and infant who
   blessed,
Each, all, are away to their dwellings
   of rest.

HE maid on whose cheek, on
whose brow, in whose eye,

Shone beauty and pleasure—her triumphs
are by;

And the memory of those who loved
her and praised,

Are alike from the minds of the living
erased.

THE hand of the king that
the sceptre hath borne;
The brow of the priest that
the mitre hath worn;
The eye of the sage and the heart of
the brave,
Are hidden and lost in the depth of
the grave.

THE peasant,
  whose lot was to sow and to reap;
The herdsman, who climbed with his
  goats up the steep;
The beggar, who wandered in search of
  his bread,
Have faded away like the grass that
  we tread.

THE saint who enjoyed the
communion of heaven,
The sinner who dared to remain
unforgiven,
The wise and the foolish, the guilty
and just,
Have quietly mingled their bones
in the dust.

So the multitude goes, like the flower
    or the weed
That withers away to let others
    succeed;
So the multitude comes, even those
    we behold,
To repeat every tale that has often
    been told.

For we are the same our fathers
    have been;
We see the same sights our fathers
    have seen;
We drink the same stream and
    view the same sun,
And run the same course our
    fathers have run.

The thoughts we are thinking our fathers
would think;
From the death we are shrinking our
fathers would shrink;
To the life we are clinging they also
would cling;
But it speeds for us all, like a bird on
the wing.

They loved, but the story we cannot
    unfold;
They scorned, but the heart of the
    haughty is cold;
They grieved, but no wail from their
    slumbers will come;
They joyed, but the tongue of their
    gladness is dumb.

They died, ay! they died: and we things
    that are now,
Who walk on the turf that lies over their
    brow,
Who make in their dwelling a transient
    abode,
Meet the things that they met on their
    pilgrimage road.

EA! hope and despondency, pleasure and pain,
We mingle together in sunshine and rain;
And the smiles and the tears, the song and the dirge,
Still follow each other, like surge upon surge.

'Tis the wink of an eye, 'tis the draught
    of a breath,
From the blossom of health to the pale-
    ness of death,
From the gilded saloon to the bier and
    the shroud,—
Oh, why should the spirit of mortal be
    proud?

Gray's Elegy.

THE curfew tolls the knell of parting day,
    The lowing herd winds slowly o'er the lea,
The ploughman homeward plods his weary way,
    And leaves the world to darkness and to me.

Now fades the glimmering landscape on the sight,
And all the air a solemn stillness holds,
Save where the beetle wheels his droning flight,
And drowsy tinklings lull the distant folds;

Save that, from yonder ivy-mantled tow'r,
The moping owl does to the moon complain
Of such as, wand'ring near her secret bow'r,
Molest her ancient, solitary reign.

Beneath those rugged elms, that yew-tree's shade,
Where heaves the turf in many a mould'ring heap,
Each in his narrow cell for ever laid,
The rude forefathers of the hamlet sleep.

The breezy call of incense-breathing morn,
The swallow, twitt'ring from the straw-built shed,
The cock's shrill clarion, or the echoing horn,
No more shall rouse them from their lowly bed.

For them no more the blazing hearth shall burn,
  Or busy housewife ply her evening care;
No children run to lisp their sire's return,
  Or climb his knees the envied kiss to share.

Oft did the harvest to their sickle yield;
  Their furrow oft the stubborn glebe has broke;
How jocund did they drive their team afield!
  How bow'd the woods beneath their sturdy stroke!

Let not Ambition mock their useful toil,
  Their homely joys, and destiny obscure;
Nor Grandeur hear with a disdainful smile
  The short and simple annals of the poor.

The boast of Heraldry, the pomp of Pow'r,
  And all that Beauty, all that Wealth e'er gave,
Await, alike, th' inevitable hour;
  The paths of Glory lead but to the grave.

Nor you, ye proud, impute to these the fault,
  If Mem'ry o'er their tomb no trophies raise,
Where, thro' the long-drawn aisle and fretted vault,
  The pealing anthem swells the note of praise.

Can storied urn, or animated bust,

    Back to its mansion call the fleeting breath?

Can Honour's voice provoke the silent dust,

    Or Flatt'ry soothe the dull, cold ear of death?

Perhaps in this neglected spot is laid
  Some heart once pregnant with celestial fire;
Hands that the rod of empire might have sway'd,
  Or waked to ecstasy the living lyre.

But Knowledge to their eyes her ample page,
  Rich with the spoils of time, did ne'er unroll;
Chill Penury repress'd their noble rage,
  And froze the genial current of the soul.

Full many a gem of purest ray serene
  The dark unfathom'd caves of ocean bear;
Full many a flow'r is born to blush unseen
  And waste its sweetness on the desert air.

Some village Hampden, that with dauntless breast,
  The little tyrant of his fields withstood;
Some mute, inglorious Milton here may rest;
  Some Cromwell guiltless of his country's blood.

Th' applause of list'ning senates to command,
 The threats of pain and ruin to despise,
To scatter plenty o'er a smiling land,
 And read their hist'ry in a nation's eyes,

Their lot forbade; nor circumscribed alone
 Their growing virtues, but their crimes confined;
Forbade to wade through slaughter to a throne,
 And shut the gates of Mercy on mankind;

The struggling pangs of conscious Truth to hide,
　To quench the blushes of ingenuous Shame,
Or heap the shrine of Luxury and Pride
　With incense kindled at the Muse's flame.

Far from the madding crowd's ignoble strife,
　Their sober wishes never learn'd to stray;
Along the cool, sequester'd vale of life
　They kept the noiseless tenor of their way.

Yet ev'n these bones from insult to protect,
　Some frail memorial still erected nigh,
With uncouth rhymes and shapeless sculpture deck'd,
　Implores the passing tribute of a sigh.

Their name, their years, spelt by th' unletter'd Muse,
　The place of fame and elegy supply:
And many a holy text around she strews,
　That teach the rustic moralist to die.

For who, to dumb Forgetfulness a prey,
  This pleasing, anxious being e'er resign'd,
Left the warm precincts of the cheerful day,
  Nor cast one longing, ling'ring look behind?

On some fond breast the parting soul relies,
  Some pious drops the closing eye requires:
Ev'n from the tomb the voice of Nature cries,
  Ev'n in our ashes live their wonted fires.

For thee, who, mindful of th' unhonour'd dead,
  Dost in these lines their artless tale relate,
If, 'chance, by lonely Contemplation led,
  Some kindred spirit shall inquire thy fate;

Haply some hoary-headed swain may say,
   "Oft have we seen him, at the peep of dawn,
Brushing, with hasty steps, the dews away,
   To meet the sun upon the upland lawn.

"There, at the foot of yonder nodding beech,
　That wreathes its old fantastic roots so high,
His listless length at noontide would he stretch,
　And pore upon the brook that babbles by.

"Hard by yon wood, now smiling, as in scorn,
　Mutt'ring his wayward fancies, he would rove;
Now drooping, woful wan, like one forlorn,
　Or crazed with care, or cross'd in hopeless love.

"One morn I miss'd him on the custom'd hill,
　Along the heath, and near his fav'rite tree:
Another came; nor yet beside the rill,
　Nor up the lawn, nor at the wood was he.

"The next, with dirges due, in sad array,
　Slow through the churchway path we saw him borne.
Approach and read (for thou canst read) the lay
　Graved on the stone beneath yon aged thorn."

THE EPITAPH.

Here rests his head upon the lap of Earth
    A youth to Fortune and to Fame unknown;
Fair Science frown'd not on his humble birth,
    And Melancholy mark'd him for her own.

Large was his bounty, and his soul sincere,
    Heav'n did a recompense as largely send;
He gave to Mis'ry all he had—a tear;
    He gain'd from Heav'n—'twas all he wish'd—a friend.

No farther seek his merits to disclose,
    Or draw his frailties from their dread abode
(There they alike in trembling hope repose),
    The bosom of his Father and his God.

THE OLD OAKEN BUCKET

The Old Oaken Bucket.

How dear to this heart are the scenes of my childhood,
When fond recollection presents them to view!

The orchard, the meadow, the deep-
tangled wildwood,
And every loved spot which my
infancy knew!

The wide-spreading pond, and the
mill that stood by it,
The bridge, and the rock where
the cataract fell,

The cot of my father, the dairy-house
    nigh it,
    And e'en the rude bucket which
        hung in the well—
The old oaken bucket, the iron-bound
    bucket,
    The moss-covered bucket which hung
        in the well.

That moss-covered vessel I hailed as
  a treasure,
  For often at noon, when returned
    from the field,

I found it the source of an exquisite
  pleasure,
  The purest and sweetest that nature
    can yield.
How ardent I seized it, with hands
  that were glowing,

And quick to the white-pebbled bot-
    tom it fell;
Then soon, with the emblem of truth
    overflowing,
    And dripping with coolness, it rose
    from the well—
The old oaken bucket, the iron-bound
    bucket,
    The moss-covered bucket arose from
    the well.

How sweet from the green mossy brim
     to receive it,
  As poised on the curb it inclined
     to my lips!
Not a full blushing goblet could tempt
     me to leave it,
  Though filled with the nectar that
     Jupiter sips.

And now far removed from the loved habitation
The tear of regret will intrusively swell

As fancy reverts
to my father's plantation
And sighs for the bucket
which hangs in the well

The old oaken bucket, the iron-bound
bucket,
The moss-covered bucket which hangs
in the well!

THE VILLAGE BLACKSMITH

The Village Blacksmith.

UNDER a spreading chestnut tree
    The village smithy stands;
The smith, a mighty man is he,
    With large and sinewy hands;
And the muscles of his brawny arms
    Are strong as iron bands.

His hair is crisp, and black, and long,
　His face is like the tan;
His brow is wet with honest sweat,
　He earns whate'er he can,
And looks the whole world in the face,
　For he owes not any man.

Week in, week out, from morn till night
You can hear his bellows blow;
You can hear him swing his heavy sledge,
With measured beat and slow,

Like a sexton ringing
the village bell,
When the evening
sun is low.

And children coming home from school
   Look in at the open door;
They love to see the flaming forge,
   And hear the bellows roar,
And catch the burning sparks that fly
   Like chaff from a threshing floor.

He goes on Sunday to the church,
   And sits among his boys;
He hears the parson pray and preach,
   He hears his daughter's voice,
Singing in the village choir,
   And it makes his heart rejoice.

It sounds to him like her mother's voice,
  Singing in Paradise!
He needs must think of her once more,
  How in the grave she lies;
And with his hard, rough hand he wipes
  A tear out of his eyes.

Toiling—rejoicing—sorrowing,
  Onward through life he goes;
Each morning sees some task begin,
  Each evening sees it close;
Something attempted, something done,
  Has earned a night's repose.

Thanks, thanks to thee, my worthy friend,
  For the lesson thou hast taught!
Thus at the flaming forge of life
  Our fortunes must be wrought;
Thus on its sounding anvil shaped
  Each burning deed and thought!